THE FIREFIGHTER BEFORE CHRISTMAS

MOLLY LIKOVICH

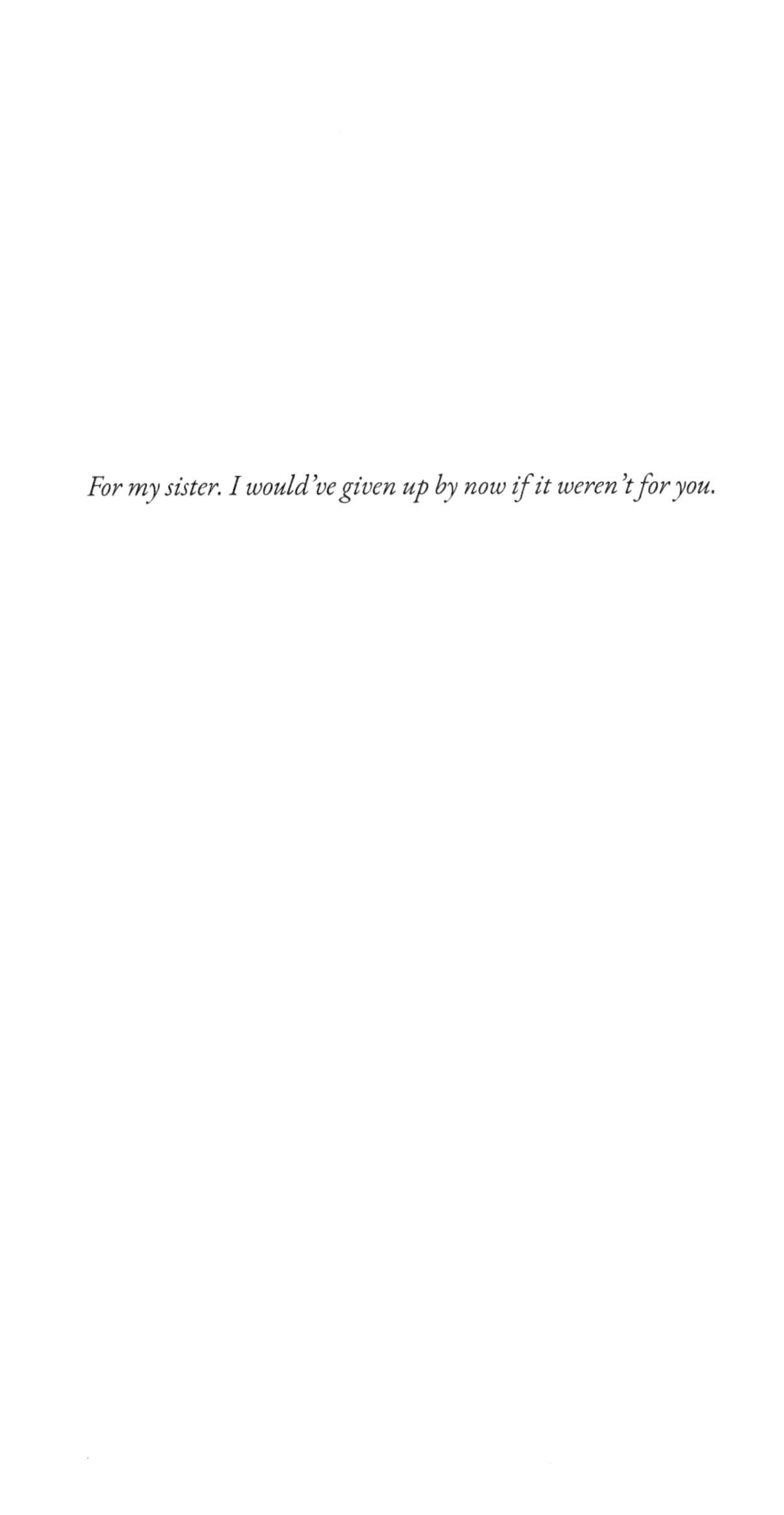

For my sister. I would've given up by now if it weren't for you.

"Pretending you're not hurt, it's not the same thing as healing."

-911

"The Befana comes at night; In worn-out shoes; Dressed as a Roman; Long live the Befana!"

-Italian Children's Song

CONTENT WARNING

This book contains depictions of depression and suicidal ideations. It also contains explicit sexual content. It is intended for readers 18+ Visit mollylikovich.com for a full list of content warnings.

Playlist

- Do You Hear What I Hear? (Celtic Woman)
- That Unwanted Animal (The Amazing Devil)
- We Need a Little Christmas (Glee Cast)
-Red (Taylor Swift)
-O Holy Night (Glee Cast)
- It's Beginning to Look a Lot Like Christmas (Michael Bublé)
- Good Grief (Bastille)
- Pompeii (Bastille)
- Enchanted (Taylor Swift)
- Don't Say You Love Me (Depeche Mode)
- Have Yourself a Merry Little Christmas (Phoebe Bridgers)
- Carol of The Bells (Pentatonix)
- Happy Xmas (The Polyphonic Spree)
- The Christmas Song (Frank Sinatra)
- Christmas Tree Farm (Taylor Swift)
-I'll Be Home for Christmas (Phoebe Bridgers)

GLOSSARY

Etruscan: The language spoken in Italy during 6 BC when it was the called Roman Italy

Ati Nanca: Etruscan for 'grandmother'

Acun: Etruscan for 'hello'

Nefts: Etruscan for 'grandchild'

Mlithuns Øu: Etruscan for 'sweet one'

La Benefa: The Good Witch of Christmas, a figure from Italian folklore

Babbo Natale: Italian for 'Santa Claus'

Haruspicy: A type of divination that involves looking at animal entrails

Sorella magic: Italian for 'sister magic'

Do You Hear What I Hear??

This is the loudest candy cane delivery I've ever heard.

The fire truck siren lets loose a stream of banshee shrieks alerting the neighborhood to the supposedly whimsical, unscheduled candy cane delivery that happens every December. The past few years it thankfully never fell on one of the nights I was babysitting Noelle. But by the cruel graces of the ancient gods tonight the city's first responders decided to provide Yuletide cheer while my sister Bobbie is off teaching her night class.

Folklore 101.

The irony.

The sirens get louder as they approach. My needle falls to the floor as I cover my ears. My eyes meet the warm ones of the taxidermy duckling in front of me. Bobbie told me not to do any more taxidermy in front of her daughter because it was 'freaking her out' but Noelle's in bed and what Bobbie doesn't know won't hurt her. But this rapidly approaching Christmas cheer might hurt my eardrums if it carries on.

"Aunt Haley!"

My four year old niece comes scurrying into the living

room, clad in her *Teenage Mutant Ninja Turtle* pajamas, her hair mussed from sleep. I shift in front of the duck to hide his half-finished bird body from her line of sight.

"The fire trucks are coming!" Noelle squeals loudly.

I nod, hands still covering my ears. "They sure are," I shout over the sirens.

Noelle beams at me and scurries over to the front door, jumping to try and reach her coat from where it dangles off the highest hook.

I groan. I swear my taxidermy duckling, Jeremy, is smirking at me.

"Aunt Haley let's go!" Noelle screeches.

The trucks are close now, I can barely hear Noelle's shrieks of joy over the blare of the jolly first responders.

"I'm coming. I'm coming."

I get up, stuff my feet into my slippers and button up my cardigan. I help Noelle into her coat then take her hand and lead her out into the chilly December night. Other children are flocking to the end of their driveways, tugging reluctant adults in tow behind them. I can see the flashing lights of the fire engines illuminating the street, an aggressive symbol of holiday cheer. Noelle tugs my arm harder until we reach the end of the driveway just as the firetruck rolls around the cul-de-sac. Noelle has her fingers in her ears but she's grinning, bouncing on the balls of her feet in anticipation. The truck makes its way to my sister's house and a firefighter hops off his perch on the steps, strong hands releasing the hand rail as he glides over to us with the poise of a dancer. He's tall. He's wearing his uniform jacket but it's unbuttoned enough that I can make out his muscles bulging against his tight uniform shirt. He's not wearing his helmet so I can perfectly see his blue eyes, shining like the winter stars, and his mouth is quirked up in a perfect smile. He has dusty blonde hair that's expertly cropped to frame his face. It's like he stepped out of a monthly calendar.

"Evening, lovely ladies," he shouts over the siren.

He takes two *tiny* candy canes out of his jacket pocket and hands them to us.

"Merry Christmas!" He keeps on smiling through the shouting.

"MERRY CHRISTMAS!" Noelle screams at the top of her lungs, fingers still in her ears.

He and I both laugh as I take the measly little candy canes from him since Noelle doesn't seem to plan on removing her fingers from her ears any time soon.

"Merry Christmas," I say at what I hope is a reasonable volume to combat the banshee behind him.

The firefighter's fingers brush against mine as the candy cane wrappers crinkle in my hand. I swear I feel a spark ignite against the winter chill from that simple, little touch. Not even a touch, just a graze. But still.

The firefighter winks at me before turning and hopping back on the truck. Amidst the flashing lights I can make out his last name printed on the back of his uniform.

CANNYN.

I wish I knew his first name, but it's too late, the banshee is already zipping down the road to deliver more miniature Christmas candies to the rest of the good little children of Huey, Maryland.

Noelle finally unplugs her ears to reach grabby fingers up towards me, silently demanding her candy. I unwrap the poor excuse for a treat and hand it to her, keeping the other one for myself. I suck on it and let the peppermint wash over my tongue as I hold onto my niece's sticky, chilled fingers, and lead her back to the house, the wail of sirens fading into the distance.

We Need a Little Christmas

Bobbie pokes at Jeremy's beak hard enough to make him wobble on his shiny, new stand.

"Would you stop it?" I demand, stirring a hot chocolate packet into my coffee. "Don't harass him."

My sister rolls her eyes. "He's dead, Haley."

"He's thriving."

Bobbie shakes her head and sips her iced coffee. "Your job is gross."

"It's art."

"Yeah, yeah, yeah. Hey thanks for taking Noelle out for the firetrucks last night."

I lean back at the counter, push my hair over my shoulder, and pick back up the scalpel to get back to work on my current project, a squirrel—Kimberly, to be precise.

"It's not exactly like I had a choice."

"You're a humbug." My sister leans over the counter. "Look at how Jiminy decorated the shop, you're going to break his heart with your severe lack of Christmas cheer."

I look up and give my sister a withering look. "He hung up a wreath on the door and one string of lights."

"That's two more things than you. Do you even have a tree in your apartment?"

"I come over to your house for Christmas. Why do I need my own tree?"

Bobbie does the bisexual iced coffee swirl before taking another sip. "Like I said, *Christmas cheer.*"

I scoff and lock back into focusing on my work.

Bobbie knows how I feel about Christmas. I don't know how she can still find any joy in it after what happened two years ago. Maybe she does it for Noelle, maybe the magic of our family line runs through her veins stronger than mine. Bobbie embodies the joy of our grandfather and I seem to possess the wandering lost soul of it all like the legends of our great-grandmother.

Bobbie checks her smart watch. "I have to get to work. My 400 class has their end of semester presentations today."

"There's a 400 level class for folklore?"

"Yes, for students who want to be folklorists like me."

"You're not a folklorist, you're a fraud."

Bobbie laughs, the sound like jingle bells, her dark hair, identically curly to mine but short enough that the curls bounce beneath her ears. "Why? Because I know it's all real?"

"Mmhmm." I scalpel some innards from Kimberly, drowning out the North Pole-ness of my sister's demeanor.

"See you for Christmas Eve dinner?"

I wave my scalpel in the air. "Yeah, yeah. As always."

"Love you."

She blows me a kiss and saunters out of the store, the cowbell above the door clanging with her departure.

Jiminy comes down to the shop around lunch time to drop off my paycheck and putter around his office, pretending like he actually still runs the place when really we both know it's just his inheritance paying the bills. An hour before closing he hobbles out of his office with his cane and taps his four-pronged tip against my derby handle walking stick from where it's propped up behind the counter.

"The cold makes my joints act up too." He chuckles.

I smirk and shake my head. My rheumatoid arthritis is a bitch when the temperature drops. During the warmer months I can manage most days without the cane and compression gloves and knee sleeves, but Jiminy's cane is a permanent fixture; makes sense seeing as he's almost ninety years old.

"Heading out, Jiminy?"

He shrugs into his winter coat and nods, tugging a floppy knit hat his late husband made for him down over his ears.

"Meeting some pals for a drink. Make sure to bundle up, Haley. The winter winds are wild tonight."

I smile and nod. "Will do, Jiminy."

He pauses for a moment, his eyes taking on a glassy look. "I worry about you, you know? All alone."

I huff. "You have no reason to worry about me. I like being alone."

We both know I'm lying. But Jiminy knows better than to push the topic with me. He gives me a kind pat on the shoulder. "You get home safe, Haley."

I give him a salute. "Always do. Until tomorrow."

He lifts his cane to me, I reach over and pick up mine, lifting it as well until they click together.

"Cane gang for life?" I ask around the widest smile I've managed in days.

"You know it." He grins around his snowy beard, setting his cane back down and leaning far more heavily against it than I ever need to lean on mine. He blows me a kiss (my second air kiss of the night) before hobbling out the door.

I sigh and turn up the Amazing Devil song on the record player to fill the space with some haunting winter tunes that aren't Christmas carols. I lose myself in my work and finish up Kimberly just as the cowbell clangs again. I look up, expecting to see Jiminy returning, having forgotten something, but instead I'm greeted by the starry eyes of firefighter Cannyn. I almost drop Kimberly on the floor at the sight of him.

"I—" I start, hands shaking as I try to hold the squirrel steady.

"Well, this certainly is a Christmas miracle," he says, approaching the desk. "I don't know if you remember me but we sort of met last night when—"

"I remember," I say quickly, cheeks flushing cherry red. "The candy canes."

He smiles, reaching the counter and resting his large, strong-looking hands on top of it. "That's right. Unfortunately, I didn't get the chance to properly introduce myself." He holds out his hand. "I'm Oliver Cannyn."

I glance down at Kimberly, her beady eyes stare at me accusingly. I set her aside on the counter and reach out to shake Oliver's hand. As I suspected, his grip is firm, his long fingers and wide palm engulfing mine so easily.

"How did you find this place?" *Jiminy's Oddities* isn't exactly a popular spot in town.

"I was a bit tenacious about the whole thing. After I saw you last night I couldn't get you out of my head so I looked up the address and found your sister's name, Bobbie Rossi. She looks a hell of a lot like you but—" he taps a finger by the corner of his eye, "—your eyes are different."

"Yeah, and—" I grab one of my long curls. "The hair."

He smirks and shrugs. "Hair can grow but those vibrant green eyes? Couldn't forget eyes like yours. So I looked your sister up on Instagram and found pictures with you and then on your profile I saw pictures of this place." He glances down at Kimberly. "Must say I didn't expect you to be a taxidermist."

"What did you expect me to be after looking at me for five seconds and handing me a candy cane?"

He chuckles. "Fair. I guess I expected you to be something more conventional."

I cross my arms over my chest, feeling irrationally defensive. "Like a mother?"

"I admit I did think you were that little girl's mother."

"I'm Noelle's aunt."

"I put that much together."

I drop my arms as quickly as I crossed them, taking in the earnest look in his eyes. I don't know why exactly it bothers me that he assumed I was a mother but I can't fault him for it, it only makes sense, I would've thought the same thing if I was in his place.

"Why put in so much effort?"

Honestly, it's not that hard to track me down. If firefighters have easy access to people's addresses and the names attached to them, it's understandable that it only took him a few Instagram clicks to locate me. Still, I've matched with guys on dating apps who don't want to put in the effort to pick the location of a coffee date or even text me first, and this near stranger put in actual time and effort to find me.

Oliver shrugs. "I wanted to talk to you. Couldn't really do that last night."

"Right." I nod. "Those candy canes weren't going to deliver themselves."

He puts a hand over his heart. "I take my sacred duty as a candy cane deliverer very seriously."

"Would you get some coffee with me? Or wine? Sparkling water? Whatever you want."

He's so damn charismatic and looks far too sexy to be such a gentleman. It staggers me.

"Uh, I like coffee," I manage to say through my what I

hope isn't embarrassingly obvious lust at first sight. "I get off in about half an hour."

His smile turns to a beaming grin. "Okay! Great! Do you know *Risers* down the street? Want to come on over and meet there when you get done?"

"Sure."

"Great." He keeps beaming. Butterflies riot to life in my stomach, their wings scraping against my ribcage as they claw their way up, begging to be set free. "See you then!" He keeps smiling over his shoulder at me as he leaves.

Once the cowbell chimes as the door closes behind him I manage to fully exhale and wait for the burning flush in my cheeks to dissipate. I put Kimberly on her shelf next to Jeremy and go through the steps of closing, making sure everything's tidy and ready for when Jiminy opens up tomorrow morning bright and early.

I grab my cane and feel briefly self-conscious. I try to get past it. Bobbie is always telling me it doesn't matter what people think about it, and then starts listing off fictional characters that in her opinion 'rock' canes: Wonka (Timotheé Chalamet's version to be precise), Lady Danbury, and Lucius Malfoy (though I'm not sure that last one is a fantastic example). But still, the idea of a sexy firefighter seeing me walk with a cane makes me feel less than beautiful, and I hate that I struggle with this internalized ableism.

Ever since that day two years ago when the brakes gave out, everything went to hell, despite how illogically cheerful Bobbie continues to be about life.

I put off getting a cane for the first year but once Jiminy found me collapsed on the floor behind the counter and learned I had been hiding my rheumatoid arthritis diagnosis from him, he and Bobbie teamed up to insist I get one.

Noelle loves my cane. She calls it Gandalf's Staff. How a four year old is so well versed in *Lord of The Rings* is a testament to what a nerd my sister is; indoctrinating her young. Whether or not that's worse than the 'jolly' indoctrination she and I faced growing up I can't say.

I leave the shop, hooking my cane over my wrist so I can lock the door, and when I turn around I'm surprised to see Oliver eagerly walking across the street to me.

"Hi." He smiles, standing before me, towering above me like an Adonis.

"I thought I was meeting you there." I awkwardly set my cane down and lean on it, my knees clicky and spasming from sitting all day.

"I know, but I realized it gets dark so early now and I didn't want to leave you to walk over by yourself." He glances down at my cane. I clench my jaw and await the ignorant comment that's sure to follow. "Are you injured?"

"No," I grind out. "I'm disabled."

"Oh, god, I'm sorry, that wasn't appropriate of me to ask, was it?"

His self-realization is a surprisingly refreshing change of pace from the usual interactions I have with able-bodied folks.

"That's okay." I offer him a small smile. "Most people ask stupid questions about it."

He hesitates, a look of unsurety in his eyes, but once he realizes I'm teasing he breaks out into a laugh and I can't help but join in.

He offers me his arm. "Shall we?"

I tuck my free hand into the crook of his elbow and allow him to lead me down the sidewalk towards *Riser's,* my cane thumping softly against the pavement. *Riser's* isn't very crowded, most of the college kids in town finished their finals earlier in the week and gone home for the holidays, and locals headed out after their shifts for some last minute shopping. Unsurprisingly, no one seems to frequent *Jiminy's Oddities* for their Yuletide gifts.

The bell at *Riser's* chimes sweetly (unlike the barnyard noise we have at Jiminy's) as we enter and I walk with Oliver over to the counter. We order peppermint mochas and he pays without even waiting for that awkward pause where the girl has to look at the guy and silently hope they'll be a gentleman. Instead, he's handing the barista his card before I've even fully had the chance to process that he had always planned to pay.

A Christmas miracle indeed.

Once we're seated with our drinks, Oliver dives right in.

"So, is Rossi Italian?"

I blow softly on the scalding drink and nod. "Yes. My parents are from Italy. Well, they're still there. My sister and I moved to America a few years ago."

"From Italy?" He quirks a brow in obvious confusion. "You got rid of your accent awfully fast."

Fuck, why did he have to start with this question? I'm nowhere near as good as Bobbie at spinning white lies to explain my heritage to non-magical folks.

"No, uh I was raised by my grandparents—" *Sort of.* "—in Greenland. "Well, a tiny island off the coast of Greenland."

"Which island?"

Jesus Christ.

"Kaffeklubben."

Otherwise known as the entrance to The Terrestrial North Pole. No people actually live on Kaffeklubben as far as any government or non-magical folk know, but that's the way my family and ancestors like it. Most people don't ask which island, and if they do they don't ever bother to go home and Google it. I'm realizing now that Oliver clearly already utilized search engines to seek me out today so perhaps letting this slip wasn't the smartest move. Maybe I can play dumb if he ever calls me out on it.

"Still no foreign accent," he points out with a smirk.

I shrug. "What can I say? I'm adaptable. Are you from Maryland?"

He sips his festive coffee. "Yes indeed. Originally from Baltimore, but moved down here for the job. Few years ago my chief had to recruit for the new firehouse and I was lucky enough to make the cut."

"Do you want to be chief one day?" I'm grateful for the topic change.

He takes another big sip of his coffee and I can't help the way my eyes are immediately drawn to his mouth.

"No, that's honestly a bit too much pressure. But I wouldn't mind being captain one day."

"What's the difference?"

"Captains are usually in charge of a single house, whereas chiefs overlook the whole show."

"I see."

"What got you into taxidermy?" He grins.

I bite my lip to hide my smile, I know he's subtly teasing. "You still think it's weird."

"It's not that I find it weird that *you* specifically do that, I find all taxidermists to be weird."

I laugh. "I get it. It's a silly origin story. I saw an animal die when I was really young—" *a reindeer* "—and I was devastated, so the idea of there being a way for one to be immortalized forever in their happy moments was beautiful to me. Not all of the animals we sell were once someone's pet, but it is a service we offer. After a while it just became an art form I really grew to appreciate. And working for Jiminy is the best. I wouldn't choose anything different."

Oliver nods. "That's beautiful."

"Did you always want to be a firefighter?"

"Yeah. My apartment burned down when I was a little kid and I nearly died from smoke inhalation. I'll never forget the firefighter that saved me that day. If it weren't for her, I wouldn't be sitting here with *this* beautiful woman right now."

Damn him. I'm blushing again.

"That's scary." There were never fires at The Terrestrial North Pole, none that weren't safely roasting chestnuts, that is. "Surviving a fire. I can't even imagine. But I guess that's your job now."

He taps his fingers against his cup but then sets one palm down flat on the table and not so discreetly begins to slide it across the surface to where one of my hands is resting beside my cup. I bite my lip again, hiding a bemused smirk. He's charming but not very smooth. It's endearing.

"It is part of my job, but we do more than just fight fires, we respond to most 911 calls really, helping with various emergencies. We have to be widely trained."

"Like rescuing cats from trees?" I tease.

Oliver smirks. "Yes, something like that."

His hand slides closer to mine. I look down again and watch as his fingers ghost across mine; my pink compression gloves covering everything but the tips, my black nail polish poking out in contrast. I wonder if he thinks I look ridiculous. I got these gloves because they match my cane and I'm a pink girly at heart. I figured if I had to wear and use all these aids then at least I could make them look a little fun.

I cave and slide my own hand across to meet his, his fingers climb up mine, nails grazing against the fabric of my gloves.

"What are these for?" he asks.

"I have rheumatoid arthritis. The cold weather makes my joints hurt like hell. These are compression gloves."

My hand twitches anxiously beneath his, as if my ailing body decided to flare up at the mere mention of my disability.

"That's awful."

I meet his gaze and can tell he genuinely means that. And unlike every other guy or girl I've gone out with since getting my diagnosis, he doesn't look horribly uncomfortable with learning details about my chronic pain.

"It is." We card our fingers together like it's second nature, as if our hands being woven together like this is what we were always meant to do. "I got into a car accident two years ago."

My brain rapidly follows up this statement with the parts I can never bear to say out loud, the intrusive thoughts that follow me around constantly but always seem to get worse around Christmas. Though it's no secret as to why. I'm immediately flooded with the memory of that night when my brakes gave out on the icy road. When Bobbie and Noelle and Christopher were in the car with me and only three of us lived to tell the tale and it's all my fault. I deserve to be in pain, it's nothing compared to all the pain I caused. If I had just stayed at The Terrestrial North Pole, none of this ever would've happened.

"I'm so sorry." Oliver squeezes my hand and it somehow lessens the pain, I suppose the extra pressure helps. "No one should have to deal with that, but especially not someone so young. What are you? Twenty-five?"

I bark out a laugh without meaning to. "You flatter me. I'm thirty."

He laughs too, but the sound is far more gentle than mine. Why am I so rough around the edges all the time? What kind of Christmas magic folk am I? A poor one, that's what kind.

Oliver squeezes my hand again before beginning to stroke his thumb back and forth across the inside of my wrist. "I'm thirty-three."

"Geez, you're practically ancient."

"Oh yeah," he laughs. "I'm like the crypt keeper."

We both laugh, the sound is sweeter than the coffee. I

might hate Christmas and the stupid candy cane delivery but I don't hate that it brought this man into my life. Maybe this is a fleeting infatuation that will be short lived, or maybe it will be something more. If it's the latter it will surely crash and burn, creating a blaze too strong for even the bravest firefighter to extinguish.

When we finish our coffees, Oliver walks me to my car and waits for me to tuck my cane and purse into the passenger seat. I turn back around to face him, hands stuffed in my pocket but I find I desperately want to reach for him. It's been so long since I've been held by someone. I feel the kind of cold that only human touch and connection can provide.

Oliver wants to touch me too but unlike me he has no reservations. He reaches out and takes the ends of my *Red* Taylor Swift scarf in his hands and pulls lightly, silently asking me to move closer.

"I'm glad I found you," he says. "I know we just met but I like you."

"I like you too."

"Can I see you again?"

Crash and burn it is.

I bite my lip again and nod. Oliver releases one hand from my scarf and brings it to my chin, his finger is chilled to the touch as he lightly runs a thumb across my mouth, pulling my lip free from my teeth.

"You should let me do that," he breathes.

My mouth parts slightly and I give the tiniest nod, so subtle that for a second I'm worried he didn't register it. But then he dips his head down and his mouth finds mine. He tastes like peppermint coffee and smells like pine needles and a light, smoky musk I suspect most of the firefighters have. I gasp against his mouth as he takes my bottom lip between his teeth, making good on his promise. I remove my hands from my pockets and bring them to his chest, pressing flat against the lapels of his coat. He takes one hand in his, the other sliding from my jaw to the back of my head where he tangles his fingers into the hair at the nape of my neck and tugs hard enough to pull another gasp from my mouth. He laughs softly against my lips before I swallow the sound and stand on tip-toe to better reach his mouth, taking his bottom lip in between my own teeth.

He groans into my mouth and moves both hands to grip my hips, pressing me up against my car, grinding into me. I move my hands to wrap around his neck, hanging from his body like a Christmas ornament. This sweet fool has me having cheery thoughts, something my own sister hasn't been able to get me to do in years.

Oliver runs his tongue along my top teeth, silently begging for entrance. I oblige him, parting my mouth wider to let his tongue slip into my mouth, the peppermint taste and pine scent further invading my senses. I can't help but moan softly against his mouth as we deepen the kiss.

"Get a room, lovebirds!"

We break apart at the sound of a group of frat boys drunkenly stumbling out of *Mike's Pub* across the street. It's not even eight yet, they must be doing their end of semester holiday bar crawl. They're all laughing and pointing at us. I glare their way as they continue to hoot and holler. Oliver moves to block my body from them and takes my chin between his thumb and forefinger, tilting my head back to meet his gaze.

"Haley."

"Yes?"

"Can I have your number?"

I hesitate for a moment before laughing. He joins in and soon the sound of our laughter drowns out the heckling of the drunken assholes down the street.

Oliver and I exchange numbers then he stands on the sidewalk and waves to me as I drive away. At the first stoplight I reach I crane my neck to peek in the rearview mirror. My lips are swollen and red as Santa's suit.

Crash and burn for sure.

O, HOLY NIGHT

La Befana is waiting for me when I arrive home. She's sitting on the couch in the corner of my studio apartment, my tabby cat, Charlie Chaplin, curled up and purring in her lap. Despite the fact that she's centuries old, she doesn't look a day over seventy. I can only hope to be so lucky (not that I'm aiming to be anywhere near as old as her, living to one or two hundred would suit me just fine).

"Acun, Nefts," *Hello, Granddaughter,* she says in ancient Etruscan.

She knows many languages, including English, Italian, and Greenlandic, but she insists so often on speaking in a language I hardly know. Since she was born back when Italy was Roman Italy, she still prefers to speak in her native language. There aren't many other beings left alive who know any Etruscan besides the random scholar or AI generated Google search, so she's left to use rogue phrases with me and Bobbie and her son Babbo Natale when she visits him (which is less and less since Bobbie and I moved away).

"Acun, Ati Nanca." *Hi, Grandma.* "Why are you here?

Don't you need to be getting ready to hunt down all the good little boys and girls of Bethlehem."

She waves me off then waves her hand towards the kitchenette just as the tea kettle begins to whistle. The kettle levitates off the burner and onto the counter where two mugs are waiting (Halloween mugs because I have self-respect).

"Pour me some tea, would you, dear?"

"Sure."

I retreat to the kitchen and pour the hot water then add two bags of chamomile tea to her mug and two bags of chai tea to mine. After adding a hefty amount of milk and sugar to both, I bring the steaming mugs over to her. I curl up next to her on the sofa. As much as my great- grandmother can irk me, I really do miss her the rest of the year.

"You don't usually show up here." She always comes to Bobbie's on Christmas Eve for family dinner and that's it.

"I missed Yule so I figured I should stop by and check on you."

"A likely story. You haven't visited on Yule since I was a kid."

"That's right." She sips her tea despite the fact that it's undeniably still scalding. She is unflinching against the heat. Of course she is, she must have cast a silent cooling charm. "Back when you and Bobbie lived where you were supposed to."

"In a cottage in the middle of nowhere Kaffeklubben?"

She scoffs. "Your pantry door led directly to your grandfather's land."

"I'm not an elf! Neither is Bobbie! We couldn't stay there forever. There was no place there for us."

"You could've come with me. You know your grandfather has doors to everywhere our family dwells. You could've gone to Italy. But no, you two chose *America*, of all places."

I scoff back at her, slumping back against the sofa. "Visit Italy? To see who exactly?"

Ati Nanca is quiet against my inquiry.

"Our parents?"

She sips her tea again. "Perhaps."

"Our parents as in the man and woman who abandoned us at the portal to The Terrestrial North Pole when they realized we were magical like you?"

Ati Nanca sighs, but she knows I'm right. My mother had hoped that since the magic of her ancestry had skipped her that it would skip her children as well. So she ran away to Italy, the land of our maternal ancestors, and met our father, a devout Christian man who took the Biblical term *thou shalt not suffer a witch to live* very seriously. She told him nothing of her magical father and grandmother, nothing of the possibility that one day new Christmas Witches would come along and follow in La Befana's footsteps. Footsteps that pre-date the terms 'Christmas' and 'Christian.'

Not that I think our mother would have been any happier having sons. Our grandfather, Babbo Natale, often spoke of wanting to train an heir and since his wife was mortal and my mother who, although she was born immortal, had no traces of magic, there seemed to be no hope of anyone to follow in Grandpa's footsteps. He always said he was 'getting tired.' But according to Ati Nanca, he's been saying that for centuries.

It truly seemed like the magic of the Rossi family would end with Babbo Natale until Bobbie and I came along. But the price of inheriting passage into a world of wonder and unimaginable magic was the loss of our parents. I don't even know if they're still alive. I barely remember them. I wonder if our father would insist the church burn us at the stake. I don't know much about how churches work these days, I avoid them at all costs.

Ati Nanca frowns, but she knows I'm right. "Well, your mother had a tendency to be a foolish woman."

"Because she listened to my father when he told her it wasn't Christian to have witches for daughters and convinced her to abandon us? Yeah, I'd say that's pretty fucking foolish."

Ati Nanca titters over the rim of her mug. I smirk but can't quite bring myself to laugh at the painful memory. My tea has finally cooled and I take a sip. My swollen lips flinching a bit from the heat.

"You're full of sorrow tonight, Mlithuns Øu." *Sweet one.*

"I'm fine."

"You are thinking about Christopher." She glances at my gloves and then over to the door where I propped my cane. "Blaming yourself as usual."

"I'm fine, Ati Nanca."

She smiles. She loves when I speak Etruscan, even if it's just the teeniest bit.

"Mmhmm. You're a very bad liar."

"Why are you here? Christmas Eve is in a few days and, as I established, you haven't visited for Yule since we moved to America."

"Yes, because I loathe America."

"You and everyone else. Get an original thought oh, great La Befana."

She chuckles and sets her mug down. She reaches into her red cloak and removes a small wooden box. She hands it to me. I take it tentatively. She doesn't usually bring me or Bobbie presents since we're not children anymore, all her family gift giving energy is showered on Noelle.

I open the box to reveal a large, teardrop pendant with an emerald in the center. My head snaps back up to meet her gaze.

"Ati—"

"This belonged to me, and well, your mother wouldn't

want such a thing, as you know. But I think you could use its power now."

"But..." I gaze back down at the stone. "Bobbie's the oldest."

"Just because Bobbie was born first doesn't mean she's the only one who deserves pretty, powerful things. Bobbie found her power easily, but we are all different—unique. I decided you could use a little extra power to guide you on your way through this dark world."

I take the necklace from its box. I shed my coat and scarf before clasping the necklace around my neck so that it can rest against my chest, the coolness of the stone seeming to provide an immediate sense of calm.

"There." Ati Nanca smiles. "A lovely Christmas gift for a lovely girl."

"You know—" I meet my great-grandmother's gaze again. "—the stories all say you wandered aimlessly and never found the Christ child that night. That you felt foolish for not going with the three wise men."

Ati Nanca laughs. "Oh, please. I'm the one who gave those three idiots directions."

It's Beginning To Look A Lot Like Christmas

I can't believe I'm doing this.

This is not the kind of thing I do.

It's so cheery, and Christmassy, and honestly the kind of thing a girlfriend would do. And I am none of those things. And still when I woke up this morning (two hours before my alarm) with Charlie Chaplin purring beside me, I knew this was what I wanted to do. I felt so deeply compelled to do it that I briefly wondered if Ati Nanca had cast a spell on me, but even she wouldn't do something so ridiculous.

I utilized my early waking to bake two dozen chocolate chip muffins. I wrapped one tray with foil to bring to Jiminy's and then I put the other dozen in a basket lined with a cloth napkin. I considered adding a bow but that seemed far too festive and I had to draw the line somewhere.

Now I'm walking up to the local firehouse with those damn butterfly wings scratching at my throat. I walk through the open garage door to see several firefighters in uniform cleaning the trucks. A young woman wearing a hijab that perfectly matches her uniform sees me first and smiles.

"I see you come bearing gifts," she stands up straight, draping the rag she was using to clean over her shoulder and walks over to me.

"Yes, um...is Oliver here?"

The other few firefighters—all men—immediately look up and start sharing looks. I feel like an animal in a zoo.

"Well how about that," the woman says. "Oliver finally brings a girl home." She holds her hand out to me. "I'm Tehzeeb and those idiots behind me are Justin, Evan, and Zayden. Oliver's in the gym. Wait here. Unless..." she hovers her hand out above the basket.

I pull the napkin back to reveal the muffins.

"Oooo." Tehzeeb picks one up and takes a big bite. "Delicious. I like you—what's your name?"

"Haley."

"I like you, Haley."

"Give me a muffin and I'll love you, Haley," one of the three men (I have no idea which one, Tehzeeb didn't make it very clear which was which when vaguely gesturing to them) calls out to me.

"Oh, hush, you," she scolds. "She brought these for Oliver." She looks back at me. "I'll go get him. Wait here."

She takes off towards the back of the station and I wait awkwardly, one hand holding the basket, the other leaning on my cane.

"So how do you know Oliver?" A white man, the tallest of the three, approaches me.

"He came to the shop where I work the other day. Actually, he delivered the candy canes the other night when I was babysitting my niece—"

The man starts laughing. "Shit, that's right, I forgot Cannyn got stuck on candy cane duty."

"Shut up, Zayden," one of the other men says. He's a bit shorter than Zayden with dark skin and locs tied up in a knot on top of his head. "Some of us like playing Santa for the kids."

The comment makes me briefly wonder what Babbo Natale would think of the firetruck candy cane delivery. He's an ostentatious man, always throwing elaborate parties at the Pole and on the other side of the portal in the island cottage for other magic folk from around the world to travel to. I still remember the year Mari Lwyd came over on Yule all the way from Wales and challenged Jonsey, the Head Elf, to a rhyme contest. Obviously Jonsey lost, which meant he ended up *very* drunk by the end of the night.

"Hi," the second firefighter says. "I'm Justin."

I let the basket handle rest in the crook of my elbow to raise my hand in an awkward greeting. "I'm Haley."

"So are you and Cannyn an item?" the third one—Evan—asks.

"Um...we got coffee last night and—"

"*And*—" Oliver comes marching out to the front of the garage with Tehzeeb trailing behind him, finishing off her muffin. "—how about you boys mind your business?"

Oliver meets my stare and my heart melts.

Who the hell have I become?

Oliver walks over to me and wraps an arm around my shoulder like it's the most obvious thing to do. He shoots a look back at the others as they all make kissy faces and light-hearted jokes. It's oddly wholesome. Oliver rolls his eyes and leads me out of the garage to the sidewalk outside. He has that same musky, pine scent and I can't seem to get enough of it. His arm is so strong and he's so damn tall, it feels good to be wrapped up in him.

"I made you these." I proffer the basket, leaning my cane against the brick wall of the station. "As a...um...early Christmas gift, I guess, or a thank you for the coffee or—" *Get ahold of yourself, Rossi.*

Oliver beams at me and takes the basket, peering inside.

"They're chocolate chip muffins, my grandma's recipe."

Really they're the elves' recipe, but he doesn't need to know that.

Oliver looks up from the basket to gaze at me with those starry eyes again.

"Tehzeeb doesn't take her baked goods lightly and she was raving about these when she found me, so I'm sure they're amazing."

I internally command myself not to blush.

"I have to get to work, but I just wanted to stop by and, I don't know. If I'm being honest I haven't done *this*—" I gesture between us. "—in a while."

He laughs. "What? Date?"

"No. Like someone enough to want to see them a second time."

He raises a teasing eyebrow but doesn't mock me for the statement. He might be too good to be true.

"I understand. It's been awhile for me too since I've felt any kind of connection with someone. We'll navigate this together. Can I take you out tomorrow night? Drinks?"

"Ah...yeah, sure."

"Great. What time do you get done?"

"I only work till lunch tomorrow so you could pick me up at my apartment, if that's okay."

Oliver reaches up with one hand to push a curl that's fallen loose from my braid behind my ear. He lets his fingers linger for a moment, letting them graze gently along my jaw as he drops my hand.

"Of course that's okay, Haley."

I'm going to choke on the butterflies.

"Okay." I smile. "I'll text you my address."

"Perfect."

He reaches for me again, this time locking his fingers

around the back of my neck and pulling me in. He leans down and his mouth finds mine. The kiss is sweet and swift, but it's enough to unmoor me.

"Until tomorrow," he breathes against my lips.

———

I arrive at work to find Jiminy dozing in the armchair in his office. I decide not to wake him and take up my post behind the front counter. Since I finished working on Kimberly yesterday, I have no new projects lined up at the moment and opt to get back into the novel I've been working my way through: *The Secret History.*

I've barely made it through a chapter before Bobbie walks through the door demanding my attention.

"You went out with a sexy firefighter last night and you didn't tell me?"

"Did Ati Nanca visit you?"

Bobbie sets a paper coffee cup down in front of me. I spin it to read the writing on the sleeve. A caramel brulee latte with an extra shot. Excellent.

"No, she didn't," Bobbie says, hoisting herself onto the counter. "I was checking in last night. Wait, did she visit you?"

"Checking in? So you mean divining." I ignore her inquiry about our great-grandmother, I don't have the energy to get into that this early in the morning. "Jesus, Bobbie, did you steal another animal liver from here again?"

Bobbie huffs. "I did that *one* time. And no I didn't. Not every time I divine does it involve haruspicy."

"Then how did you know that I—"

She taps the center of my forehead with her pointer finger and then taps the center of her own forehead. "Sorella magica."

Sister magic.

Ever since we were little kids, Bobbie and I have had a deeper connection to each other than I've witnessed from other magic folk, even other sisters. Ati Nanca says it's because we possess the ancestral magic of La Befana. Regardless of why we have it, Bobbie's has always been stronger than mine when she chooses to hone in and focus on it. She's a master of all types of divination (even the less than appealing kinds that involve smuggling out animal livers from my place of employment), and therefore our spiritual connection seems to always be stronger on her end of the tether that ties our souls together. While I'm able to parse out her mood or general sense of safety she's able to pick out and focus in on incredibly detailed specific aspects of my life. It's like she's communicating with a satellite phone and I'm working with nothing but a tin can and some twine.

"Why were you checking in?" I ask.

She sips some of her coffee before answering. "You seemed sad."

"It's almost Christmas."

"You need to let that go. It's been two years."

"He was your husband, Bobbie," I insist. "I don't understand how *you* can let it go."

Bobbie frowns. "You think I let him go?" Her voice is suddenly soft, her usual bravado immediately dissipated in the silent space between us. "He was my whole world. But then Noelle came along and she became both of our whole worlds. I didn't *let him go,* I forced myself to carry on. To keep living. For my daughter, for you, for *myself.*"

I drop my gaze down to the counter, unable to look her in the eyes when I know they're full of tears she usually never sheds.

"Haley, you couldn't control the brakes giving out. You couldn't control black ice on the road. You didn't do anything wrong."

I sniff back tears of my own. "Because of me you don't have a husband, Noelle doesn't have a father, and I—" I lift up my hands, still clad in my pink compression gloves. "—have this."

Bobbie studies my hands, forever in pain, then looks me head on, tears trickling from the corners of her eyes as she takes my hands in hers.

"No one blames you for that day but you. Christopher was your friend, he wouldn't want you to live like this. This can't be the only reason you hate Christmas."

You're right, I think to myself. *It's because of all the Christmas cards I sent to Italy that our mother sent right back. It's because the only person I ever fell in love with telling me she could never marry a witch. It's because we came here and you found true love and a perfect life and I found nothing but taxidermy and loneliness.*

"I don't hate Christmas," I lie instead. "I'm just not a holiday person."

"That's bullshit. I've seen you on Halloween."

I open my mouth to respond but Jiminy's voice saves me from having to continue this line of questioning when he calls out from his office:

"Is that Miss Bobbie Rossi I hear out there?"

"It's me, Jiminy!" Bobbie calls back, swiping away the tear stains on her cheeks.

Jiminy comes walking out of his office without his cane, holding the plate of muffins I left on his desk.

"Look at the lovely gift your sister brought me," he tells her. "She's such a dear, always looking after me."

Bobbie gives my boss a warm smile before glancing back at me. Thanks to our sorella magica I know that her true feelings don't match her smiling face at all.

"She's a good one," Bobbie says to Jiminy. She hops off the counter and picks up her coffee. "I've got to get going. Lots of shopping to do and final papers to grade to be ready for the kids when they get back. Have a good day, you two."

"Goodbye, dear!" Jiminy waves to my sister before setting the plate down and picking up a muffin. "Don't let me eat all of these, Haley. I'll end up losing the rest of my teeth if I do."

I chuckle and take a muffin for myself. I've barely gotten the bottom wrapper off before my phone buzzes with a text from Bobbie.

> I expect details about the firefighter at Christmas Eve dinner with La Befana.

I munch on the muffin before responding, getting crumbs across my screen as I type.

> La Befana knows the details. She was at my apartment last night.

The typing dots pop up immediately.

> Why was she there? She hasn't come before Christmas Eve in years.

> I know. She was there to harass me. Runs in the family.

· · ·

I touch the pendant at my throat, the sensation of rubbing it between my fingers making me feel a bit calmer in the wake of my sister's interrogation. If Bobbie noticed the new necklace, she didn't mention it, thank gods. I can only handle so much traumatic turmoil for one holiday season. Having to explain to my older sister why our powerful, ancient ancestor bestowed this powerful, magical family heirloom onto me and not her is not the kind of conversation I want to have over cups of spiked eggnog. Or ever.

Let Your Heart Be Light

Oliver arrives at 8pm and my heart stops when I open the door. He's standing there in worn blue jeans, a heather gray knit sweater under a black peacoat. His blonde hair is perfectly tousled and his mouth is begging to be kissed. I'm wearing a loose pink dress over simple black tights, with a thick black cardigan. My curly hair is loose over my shoulders and Ati Nanca's necklace dangles around my throat.

"Wow," Oliver says softly. "You're beautiful."

"Thank you." I smile. "You clean up pretty nice yourself."

"Oh! Almost forgot, I brought you something." He reaches into his pocket and takes out a big candy cane with a green ribbon tied around it. "Candy cane delivery."

I laugh as I take the candy. "Well, it's not quite the same without the ear-splitting sirens, but it'll do." I unwrap the candy and pop the end in my mouth, smiling around the stem.

He smiles back and offers me his hand. "Ready?"

I grab my cane and wave goodbye to Charlie Chaplin before taking Oliver's hand and following him out into the cold. He opens the door to his pickup for me like a tried and true gentleman. He syncs up his phone with the bluetooth and Bastille plays through the speakers.

"I love Bastille," I say.

He shoots an excited smile my way before turning his eyes back to the road. "Really? What's your favorite song?"

"Good Grief."

He smiles without taking his eyes off the road.

"What's yours?" I ask.

"It's a basic answer, but Pompeii. I've been obsessed with it ever since I heard it for the first time."

"What's your favorite lyric from it?"

We come up to a red light and Oliver glances my way again. "That's a good question."

"Do you have a good answer?"

"You might again accuse me of being basic but—"

"I didn't accuse you the first time. I love Pompeii."

He smiles brighter. "The line: 'How am I gonna be an optimist about this?' has always stuck with me."

"That's not basic, that's the theme of that entire album."

"What about you?" he asks as the light turns green. "What's your favorite lyric from Good Grief?"

"'What's gonna be left of the world when you're not in it?'"

His smile softens a bit. "That's a great lyric."

We reach *Mike's Pub* and Oliver conquers the impressive feat of parallel parking, a skill most small town Marylanders don't possess (including me). He holds the door to the pub open for me and even pulls out my stool at the bar. It shows how low the expectations are for men of my generation that I'm apparently so easily wooed by these common courtesies.

The bartender, Ali, a chirpy goth who sings in a Depeche Mode cover band here most weekends, comes over and asks for our order.

"I'll just do a glass of merlot." He sets down his card. "And whatever the lovely lady's having."

Ali shoots me an impressed look.

"I'll have a glass of prosecco."

"Coming right up." Ali takes Oliver's card and starts a tab, delivering it back to him with our drinks.

"How long have you lived in Maryland?" Oliver asks, raising his wineglass to his lips.

"About seven years. We moved here when my sister was twenty-five."

"What made you want to leave Greenland?"

There's no suspicious tone in his voice which is a relief, it means he most likely didn't go home and Google Kaffeklubben.

"Things were getting...suffocating at home. We wanted to strike out on our own."

"And you chose Huey, Maryland?"

"We wanted somewhere quiet. Somewhere small and welcoming that we could call our own. We like it. My sister, Bobbie, works at the university. She teaches folklore."

"That's interesting."

You have no idea.

"So do you like it here?" he asks. "Is it what you wanted?"

"It is." I take a big gulp of my drink.

Could anywhere really be what I wanted anymore? Huey, Maryland was everything to me once. When we first moved here it was magical and new and we were happy. I had just met Jiminy and gotten into studying taxidermy professionally and Bobbie was working on her education. We met Christopher at an open mic night on the university campus and for him and my sister it was love at first sight. Then a few years later Noelle was born and all of our lives changed for the better. I was still lonely but not in the aching, awful way I was back home. I managed to stop thinking constantly about my absentee mother, about my lost elfen love, and the heavy weight of inheriting the magic of La Befana.

Ati Nanca trained us a bit growing up, but overall she said that our magic was something that the old gods would guide us through. Then, as the years went by I watched my sister's magic bloom and mine remained the same. I knew in theory I was powerful, it was the reason my mom didn't want me, but I could never seem to make that theory take life.

Bobbie and La Befana said my self-loathing was holding me back.

I say it's the chronic pain.

And chronic sadness.

"Have you worked at Jiminy's the whole time?" Oliver asks, pulling me from the dregs of my thought spiral.

"I met him shortly after we moved here when I first went into his shop. We hit it off. He spent a few years helping me study and progress in the craft and then eventually he hired me. Honestly, he's my best friend, as strange as that sounds."

Oliver shakes his head. "It's not strange. I think it's sweet. Once we're all out of our twenties I don't think age matters too much."

"I completely agree."

Especially since the relative I have the closest relationship with was alive to see the birth of Christ.

We order a second round of drinks and I'm reminded why I rarely drink. My cheeks flush, my joints flame, and my brain stops reminding my mouth to have a filter.

"Is it terrifying?" I blurt out. "Being a firefighter?"

Oliver gazes at me as he swivels in the seat of his bar stool to face me. His knees graze against mine and he settles one hand on top of my knee, fingers digging lightly into the fabric of my tights. I feel his touch like a wild blaze throughout my body, especially between my legs. I fight the urge to clench my thighs to alleviate the immediate desire I feel for him. With him this close and his hand on my leg, he would no doubt be able to tell if I was shifting to hide such a thing.

"Sometimes." He rubs his thumb lightly along the inside of my knee, moving up along my thigh and the blaze inside me burns brighter. "But then I remember how terrifying the world would be without firefighters, how many valuable lives would be lost. I remind myself every time I feel afraid that I've survived all of my worst days before and I can survive another, especially if it means the people I'm helping get to keep on surviving too."

I rest my hand on top of his. "Are you afraid of anything, Oliver?"

"Honestly?"

I nod, wrapping my fingers up with his. "Honestly."

"Being alone at the end."

Fuck.

"What about you, Haley?"

I squeeze his hand. "The same exact thing."

We lock eyes a moment longer. Time stops. We're the only two people in the bar. I feel cliche and silly and like I want to mock myself for feeling so deeply so quickly for a man I barely know, but it's like suddenly all the Taylor Swift love songs us Rossi women constantly play finally make sense. How does that one Noelle loves so much go? *I was enchanted to meet you.* Yeah, that's it.

"Do you wanna get the bill?" I ask softly.

Oliver grins and nods.

All Seem To Say Throw Cares Away

Oliver walks me to my door and I've barely turned the key in the lock before I spin around and invite him inside.

"Are you sure?" he asks. "I don't want you to feel like you have to do anything you don't—"

"Oliver." I reach up and gently take a hold of one of his lapels. "You're a true gentleman, and it's amazing, and I really, really like it, but I also *really* want you to come inside. If that's alright with you?"

"Oh, sweetheart, it's more than alright."

I turn my key the rest of the way and push my door open. We've barely crossed the threshold before he's picking me up. I drop my cane and my purse and wrap my arms and legs around him. He kicks the door closed and I fumble for the lock but it's hard to find it with my eyes closed and mouth pressed up against his.

Oliver walks me over to the bed with ease. I don't think I've ever been with someone so effortlessly strong. My core heats up with every step, every kiss, every press of his fingers and swipe of his tongue in my mouth. He sets me down on the bed, kicks off his boots, and climbs on top of me. I spread my legs to make space for him between my thighs, his hips rest against mine like they were always meant to be there.

He gently pushes some of my hair out of my face, his rough and calloused hands tracing stars along my cheeks.

"You're so beautiful, Haley."

He kisses my forehead, my jaw, the spot on my neck just below my ear that completely undoes me. I sigh and wrap my arms around him tight, digging into the thick fabric of his coat.

"We're wearing too many clothes," I breathe.

He chuckles and shifts back on his knees. I watch with rapt attention as he takes off his coat, sweater, and shirt, bearing his perfectly chiseled chest. If my thighs weren't currently spread around him I would definitely need to clench them because the sight of him shirtless has me completely wet.

I shift to try and sit up and reach for his belt buckle but he presses a hand to my shoulder and pushes me back down. I keep my eyes locked on him, speaking silent questions into existence. He shoots me a mischievous smirk then slides his hands up my thighs to hook his thumbs inside the waistband of my tights.

"Lift your hips for me, sweetheart."

I inhale softly and do as he says. We keep our eyes locked the entire time he slides my tights down my legs and tosses them onto the floor. He runs his hands back up my legs, fingers digging roughly into my thighs, thumbs gliding closer and closer to my core. He reaches my underwear and I can hear the low hum in his throat as he drags his thumb across and can feel the wetness seeped into the fabric. He continues to rub his thumb back and forth, swiping it perfectly across my clit, sending shivers and twitches through my body even with the fabric separating his finger from my bare sex.

Oliver hums low again then moves his hands to push my

dress up, exposing my stomach. He dips down and presses a kiss just below my belly button before beginning to trail kisses lower and lower until he reaches the edge of my panties. He takes the tiny silk bow stitched into the elastic in between his teeth and pulls lightly. He keeps fingers into the soft skin of my thighs, making me feel greedy with want—his mouth so close to where I want it but still so far.

I reach a hand down to tangle in his hair and tilt my hips up. "Oliver, please."

He looks up at me through starry eyes. "Please what?"

"Please put your mouth on me."

I can see how my words make him wild, a flame burns bright in his gaze. He yanks my underwear down my legs and adds it to where my tights lay on the floor. His hands spread my legs wide and then he devours me. He doesn't start slow and tentative like most guys, he feasts on me, plunging his tongue in deep then dragging it up to my clit and lightly biting down with his teeth causing my back to bow off the bed and my fingers to tighten in his hair as a moan falls free from my lips.

Just when I think I'm going to go mad from the sensation of Oliver's tongue and teeth and lips he adds two fingers to his ministrations and insanity consumes me. I cry out, not caring if my neighbors hear me, grinding my hips against his hand as his teeth continue to nip at my clit. I think I moan his name, I think I gasp the word 'please', for all I know I start to speak Etruscan. My orgasm racks my entire body, bones shaking beneath my skin while constellations take shape behind my eyes.

Oliver moves back again and grabs at the hem of my dress. "Please take this off."

I shift forward and pull my dress up and over my head, tossing it to our growing pile of clothes on the floor. In a matter of seconds Oliver undoes my bra strap and I unbuckle his belt, sliding it free of the loops and pulling down his zipper. I slide my hand down beneath the layers of fabric that separate my hand from his cock. I take him in my hand and move down his shaft, savoring the way his eyelids flutter closed and a groan escapes him. He pushes his underwear and jeans down his hips, his full erection springing free. I try not to get distracted by the size of him, eager to feel it inside me. While I continue to work him up and down, he reaches out and cups one of my breasts, lightly twisting my nipple between his thumb and forefinger. I use my free hand to press his hand closer to my chest.

"Harder," I breathe.

Oliver leans forward and lets his forehead rest against mine as his lips ghost above my mouth.

"Do you like a little pain, sweetheart?"

I smile against his mouth. "Just a bit, firefighter."

"Say less." The corners of his mouth lift up, he twists my nipple harder, I close my fingers tighter around his cock and we both moan.

"Do you have a condom?" I gasp against his lips.

Oliver nods, nose grazing mine. He gets off the bed and removes the rest of his clothes. He fishes a condom out of the pocket of his jeans and I watch as he tears open the wrapper and slides the condom on, the material spreading taut against his length. He starts to climb back on top of me but I press my palm to his chest.

"Can I be on top?" I ask.

"Of course," he says through a smile.

I shift to climb on top of him. He rests his hands on my hips to help keep me steady as I lift myself up to center my entrance over him. We lock eyes again and I slowly lower myself onto his shaft. He groans and I gasp loudly, basking in the way he stretches and fills me up so wonderfully. I wait until I'm seated to the hilt to begin to move, rocking my hips back and forth. Oliver meets my every movement, hands gripping my hips, helping move my body back and forth. I plant my hands flat on his chest and press down as I lean forward over him. My hair falling over my shoulders, curtaining my face, my breasts bouncing with each thrust.

Oliver reaches up to push my hair out of my face, running his fingers through my curly tresses before knotting his fingers into a fist and pulling tight. I hiss softly from the pain but enjoy it nonetheless. His other hand takes my other breast and his fingers begin to tease the nipple same as he did before, but this time he doesn't wait for me to tell him to do it harder, he gets to work pinching and twisting and more moans fall free from my lips like raindrops in a storm.

"You're so fucking beautiful, Haley."

I drop my head down, his fist pulling at my hair, and kiss him as we rock harder and harder. Oliver grunts against me and shifts, rolling us over onto our sides. He hooks my leg over his hip, his other hand still holding my hair. He moves the hand on my leg around to knead my ass as he slides his cock deep inside me, hitting a sweeter spot from this new angle. I let my head fall back into the force of his hand in my hair and whimper from the sensation of him thrusting into me.

"Oliver," I murmur through a pathetic mewl. "Please don't stop."

"Believe me, Haley, I have no intention of doing so."

He moves his hips harder and harder and I do my best to meet him thrust for thrust but eventually he's holding me so tight and moving so fast that all I can do is give myself over to the freedom of letting him claim my body.

"I'm so close," I gasp, hands gripping his shoulders.

He pushes into me as hard as he can and I cry out again as another orgasm decimates me. Oliver keeps pounding into me, chasing his own euphoria. He finally releases my hair and I'm able to let my head fall forward to rest in the crook of his neck.

I kiss the tendons in his neck as he fucks me to completion, his body shuddering against mine as he finishes.

For a few moments we lay there tangled up in each other, catching our breath, before he finally pulls away and smiles down at me.

"Fucking hell, Haley. You're incredible."

I laugh softly. "You're not so bad yourself."

He laughs too, pushing a lock of my now tangled curls behind my ear.

I grow quiet, everything we just did washing over me.

"What's wrong?" he twirls one of my curls around his finger.

"I just...I know it's weird for me to like rough sex when I'm..." I glance across the room to my discarded cane. "You know."

Oliver follows my line of sight before shifting to prop himself up on one elbow, bright blue eyes gazing down at me.

"It's not weird to enjoy a pain you can control."

His words relax me, my muscles loosen, my jaw unclenches. I move closer to him, letting him wrap me up in his arms and together we drift off to sleep as the snow falls outside.

And So This Is Xmas
For The Weak And
The Strong

I wake up to an empty bed and a horrible pain flare up.

I've barely opened my eyes before tears cloud the edges of my vision. I turn my head, trying not to cry out from the stabbing sensation that travels down the tendons into my arms and hands, making my fingers twitch and spasm with pain. There's a note on the nightstand. I breathe in deep then sit up and shift over across the bed, crying out in agony as the pain ricochets through the rest of my body; burning knees, knives in the tips of my toes, tight and inflamed lower back, pain blooming behind my temples. I snatch the note up.

Had to get to my shift, wanted to let you sleep. Text me later, sweetheart. ♡ *Oliver*

I shouldn't feel so hurt by the note. He had to get to work. It's not like he knew sex would cause a pain flare, it's not like I stopped to consider that last night when I was so entranced by his body, it's not like I even explained to him what a pain flare actually is and how it works.

Still…

The loneliness spreads across me like water until I'm submerged in Ophelia-sadness.

I check the time on my phone. I need to get to work too. My body screams at me that this isn't a good choice, but I hate calling out. It makes me nervous to leave Jiminy alone at the shop. He comes in every day with aching joints and a wobbly cane, so why can't I do the same?

Like so many days before this one, I clench my jaw and force myself out of bed, silently crying through the pain as I make my way to the bathroom. I struggle through my morning routine, take four ibuprofens, and slather my joints in the topical CBD cream Bobbie picks up for me whenever she goes to get vape refills. I slide compression braces over my knees, my left elbow, and my hands, bundle up against the nipping cold, and resign myself to a terrible day ahead.

What a jolly holiday indeed.

———

In a cruel twist of fate, it's unusually busy at the shop today. Granted most customers opt to buy our antique jewelry, strange gothic home decor, or the hand-crafted notebooks Jiminy's friend Marbon makes, but there are a few brave souls who venture into the taxidermy section. Only one of the few dares to make a taxidermy purchase.

Ali The Bartender.

"Hi, Haley." She sets Kimberly down on the counter.

I decked Kimberly out in a tiny, hand-knit sweater from the cloth goods part of the shop, and a little silver thimble in place of a hat. She looks rather dapper in my opinion. When we do manage to make a taxidermy sale, it's usually Jiminy's projects that sell the most, so I can't help but preen a bit under the excitement of *my* stuffed squirrel being the one a shopper selects.

"Hi, Ali." I smile and start gingerly wrapping up my creation. "Christmas gift for someone?"

Ali nods. "My partner, they're getting really into this kind of thing. I remembered you saying this place had some good stuff. Work and life have gotten so busy I ended up cutting it a bit close with shopping for gifts this year. I'm relieved you had this one. It's great."

"Thank you." I beam and finish wrapping the squirrel. "I worked hard on her. Glad she's getting a nice home. Do you want a gift box?"

"Wait, *you* did this? I thought the old guy did all the taxidermy. That's so cool, Haley!"

Ali smiles, seeming genuinely impressed by my craftsmanship. Since Bobbie and Noelle tend to find my profession rather gross, it's nice to hear someone other than Jiminy praise my work.

"Yeah, it's mine. Jiminy taught me a few years ago. He's still way better at it than me but—"

"Haley's too modest." Jiminy comes out from his back office, a bowl of Christmas chocolates balanced in his shaking hand, the other one gripping the cane. "Hello, Ali. Care for a little sweet treat?"

He offers the bowl and Ali smiles back warmly as she plucks one out. "Thanks, Jiminy. And you're right." She glances back at me. "Haley *is* too modest. This squirrel is great."

"Her name's Kimberly," I say.

"Kimberly?"

"Haley names all the creatures in here," Jiminy explains. "Just last week we sold a Ronald, a Patricia, and a Legolas."

Ali raises a bemused brow. "Legolas?"

"My niece named him," I explain. "My sister corrupted her. So, do you want a gift box?"

Ali laughs and nods. I place the tenderly wrapped squirrel into the box and tie a satin red ribbon around it before sliding it across the counter to Ali and telling her the somewhat ridiculously high cost she owes for my little, fuzzy, undead creation. Luckily, Ali's a small-time artist too and understands the value of another creator's work. She doesn't complain like so many do when checking out here.

"Thanks so much." Ali pops the candy Jiminy gave her into her mouth. "Both of you," she says around a mouthful of milk chocolate. "Happy Holidays!"

"Happy Holidays!" Jiminy and I say back in unison, his tone a bit cheerier than mine.

"Well, Haley, I'm feeling a bit more tired than usual. I'm to go upstairs and rest. Just for a little bit. You come wake me if you need anything, you hear?"

I smile and nod. "You got it."

Jiminy lovingly pats my shoulder and heads off for the stairs in the back corner of the shop that lead to his apartment upstairs.

The shop quiets down, customers stop coming, and the early evening sets in. I put on Bastille and listen to my favorite song by them over and over.

What's gonna be left of the world if you're not in it?

I've thought about leaving this world more than once in my life.

My mind travels back to years growing up at The Terrestrial North Pole among the elves and fairies and wizards like Babbo Natale. Bobbie and I were always the only witches around unless La Befana came to visit. Even then she didn't stay for very long, she made the other magic folk nervous. It never seemed fair to me that Babbo Natale and men like him could choose to call themselves wizards instead of witches and suddenly garner the respect and acceptance us witches only ever seemed to find amongst ourselves. But there were a few individuals who deigned to talk and spend time with me and Bobbie.

Images of Jenua's face flash through my mind. Her pink lips, her lavender eyes, the way her cupid's bow looked when she laughed. The way she tasted on my tongue as her thighs clenched around my head, our limbs tangled together in the early hours of the morning during the off season when she didn't have to be at the bakery first thing.

Gods, did I love her.

I asked her to marry me. I was so certain life at the Pole could be something I could endure if only she would endure it by my side. Or maybe I was really just holding out lofty hopes that she would run away with me. Cross through the portal in the cottage, go away somewhere in Greenland, or Italy, or America.

I care about you, Haley, but what would my parents think if I said I was marrying a witch? I'm sorry. I just can't.

Words that burned their way onto my heart, a scar that never faded.

It was Bobbie who saved me from myself that winter. She came into my room where I was curled up in bed surrounded by all the Christmas cards my mother returned, unopened, love letters from Jenua, old, leather tomes full of stories about wicked witches.

Let's leave this place, she told me. *For good.*

We packed our bags that night. Instead of leaving behind a suicide note, we left a goodbye letter.

We never returned. Babbo Natale still sends us Christmas gifts and letters and asks us to come home, but I think he knew all along that one day we would leave. Christmas Town is no place for people like us. Ati Nanca realized that as soon as her son began to build a land the human world came to know as a realm of childhood wonder; a fantasy world unfit for mere mortals.

I touch the pendant at my chest, the cool, calming aura radiating off it with a soft thrum. The music stops playing and without thinking I wave my finger in the air, changing the record without getting up. I gasp softly. I rarely do little magic. The silly, subtle kind of everyday tasks. I did it often when I was younger, but once Bobbie and I moved her we knew we had to get our immediate instinct to solve every issue with magic under control. It wasn't like we could walk down the street waving our wands every time we needed to mend a tear in our tights or fix our car troubles. Bobbie almost never does easy magic at home, stating that she wants Noelle to learn to do everything the mortal way and only save magic for the 'important' stuff.

After the car crash, I hoped my magic could heal me. When I failed to do so, I sought out La Befana, thinking surely such an ancient, powerful witch could take away my chronic pain. It turns out even intense healing magic can only go so far. My body remained broken and I remained sorrowful.

My phone buzzes from across the counter. I pick it up to see if it's a text from Oliver, but it's just a Duolingo reminder to practice my Italian. I sigh and tuck it away in my pocket.

I smell smoke.

It's coming from upstairs.

It's almost closing time.

I reach for my purse under the counter but of course I don't have my wand, I so rarely use it, saving it as a conduit for ritualistic magic. But even my weak intuition is telling me that not bringing it with me today was a mistake. I race up the stairs, ignoring the way my joints scream and shake in protest. Jiminy left the door unlocked in case I needed him and I burst in to see Jiminy asleep in his recliner, the stove on fire and the flames have quickly spread to the curtains, the ceiling—*everywhere.*

"Jiminy!"

I raise my hands to face the flames and try to calm them but the fire is blazing and with the way my pain flare up is already draining my strength and stamina it's becoming damn near impossible to focus my magic on such a monumental task.

You're the descendent of La Befana, I tell myself. *Get it together.*

I look back over at Jiminy, still asleep, ignorant to the immediate danger, and rush to his side. I may not be able to stop the fire but I'll be damned if I don't save him.

I fall to my spasming, aching knees and shake him awake. "Jiminy! Jiminy, you've got to wake up!"

Jiminy comes to with a startled grunt just as a blazing beam falls, pieces of roof crashing through, a wall of fire now blocking our path to the door.

"H–Haley?" Jiminy's voice is full of fear.

"It's okay. Come on, we've got to go." I grab his arm and help him to his feet. I look around frantically until I spot a somewhat clear path to the window that overlooks the back street. "This way."

Jiminy leans on me for support as we stumble, coughing horribly, through the wreckage. Jiminy weakly gestures to the burning pan on the stove.

"I'm so sorry," he whispers. "I was making dinner and—"

"It's alright, Jiminy. Just focus on me. I'm going to get you out of here."

We reach the window and it takes all my strength to open the creaky, sticky, old thing. I lean out and take in how far a drop it is to the ground. Too much for an elderly man to make. Too much for anyone to make without seriously injuring themselves. I turn back to face Jiminy. He's terrified.

I can feel Bobbie's *sorella magica* tingling through my body. Her spirit is calling out to me. I do my best to convey clearly back to her that we're in danger.

Then I remember that mortals still have systems to utilize during times like this.

I get my phone out of my pocket.

"911, what's your emergency?"

"Help!" I cough again as Jiminy slumps against the window. "I'm in the apartment above Jiminy's Oddities downtown, it's on fire! There's no way out!"

"Alright, ma'am," the dispatcher says. "Just stay calm for me, help is on the way. Now is there—"

She keeps talking but I know whatever she's saying isn't going to work. Help isn't going to get here in time. I look at Jiminy, he's going to pass out soon and there won't be any coming back from that, not with his poor health, the smoke is already too much for him. I look down at the phone and then my wrist spasms and the phone falls from my fingers, crashing to the floor, the screen cracking. The dispatcher's voice comes out muffled against the blaze of the fire. I keep looking at my hands.

I can help.

I can save him.

"Jiminy." I take his hands in mine. "I'm going to get you out of here. It's going to sound insane but you have to trust me, okay? Can you do that?"

Jiminy squeezes my hands, his teary eyes gazing into mine. "I'll always trust you, Haley. I'm so sorry, you're too young to—"

"Shut up! Just focus, alright? I promise I can get you out of here." I let go of his hands and move back to the window. "Come on." I hold my hand out to him again. He takes it, uncertainty in his eyes but then he looks down, he can see the light, crimson sparks radiating from my fingertips.

"Oh, Haley," he whispers. "I always knew it."

He smiles at me and for the first time in my life I don't feel ashamed or embarrassed to be a witch. I sniffle back tears and choke a bit on the smoke.

"I haven't done anything like this since I was a kid," I tell him. "When Bobbie and I were climbing a tree and her foot slipped I caught her then and I didn't let her fall. I won't let you fall now."

"Haley, you shouldn't worry about me. You're so young and I'm—"

"My best friend. So don't think I'm going to let you die here when I have the power to save you. I'm magic enough to get us both down from here, but you're going first, got it?"

Jiminy's warm smile falters for a moment but then he nods. I help him over the window pane, his legs dangling over the edge, smoke billowing out around us.

"Ready?" I ask him.

"Ready."

"Once you're on the ground, get to the front of the shop and wait for the firefighters. I'll meet you down there."

He looks back over his shoulder to meet my stare once more. I know he's about to change his mind and insist I conserve my energy and only save myself, but I would rather die than leave him behind knowing there was a chance I could've saved him.

So I push.

Jiminy gasps as his body begins to plummet towards the pavement below.

I thrust out my arms, hands facing down, crimson sparks shooting from my fingertips and the lines in my palms. The sparks envelop him like a life raft at sea. My knees shake, my pain flare burns as viciously as the blaze consuming Jiminy's apartment. I scream, my legs begging to buckle beneath me, but I can't stop, not until Jiminy's safe.

Finally, his feet touch down softly, gently, perfectly on the ground.

The magic has drained me. Maybe if I had been having a low symptom day I would've had enough strength left to get myself down. But neither Ati Nanca, Bobbie, or fucking Santa Claus himself are disabled, none of them live with agonizing chronic pain. The only thing their magic ever has to combat is their own minds. I can't do this anymore. My body won't hold me up, my spark is flickering out.

"Haley!" Jiminy calls up to me, but his voice sounds like it's a thousand miles away.

My body gives out.

I collapse to the floor and let the fire consume me.

I don't know how much time passes. I can hear the 911 dispatcher's voice still muffled from far away. I have no idea where my phone got to. I hope Jiminy got to the first responders in time.

A banging, crashing sound fills the space. I turn my head and blink through the hazy, fiery room to see what looks like a monster coming towards me.

No, not a monster.

A firefighter.

A very tall firefighter.

He kneels down beside me and presses an oxygen mask to my face. I inhale breathable air, gasping and crying from the sting of the smoke in my eyes and lungs.

The firefighter is talking around their own mask, the sound cloaked and covered up by the barrier between us. I manage to make out his face as he carries me through the blaze back towards the doorway.

Oliver.

He races me down the staircase, flames licking up the side, and out through the shop where the fire has begun to engulf every oddity on the shelf.

I'm glad Ali bought Kimberly, is the only somewhat cohesive thought that makes its way through my mind as Oliver carries me out of the building and into the freezing December night.

There are sirens and people shouting and someone sobbing.

Oliver sets me down on the sidewalk and waves to the paramedics. He pulls his mask off and I let my own fall away.

"Oliver," I rasp.

"Jesus Christ, Haley." He has tears in his eyes as he caresses my cheek with his gloved hand, ash stains both of our skin.

"Haley!"

I look across the street, through the crowd of spectators to see Bobbie come racing over to me. She throws herself down beside me and wraps her arms around my neck, her sobs shaking both of us.

"Thank the gods," she cries into my singed hair. "I thought I lost you."

I raise a weak hand up to hold onto one of her arms banded around me. "It's alright," I whisper. "I'm still here."

She pulls back to look at Oliver and I can tell she realizes immediately who he is.

"Thank you," she says through hiccups as she tries to compose herself. "Thank you for saving my sister."

"You don't need to thank me," he tells her, but he keeps his eyes on me. "I would do anything for her."

"Ma'am, we need to get your sister checked out," a female paramedic says, lightly touching Bobbie's shoulder.

Bobbie nods, looking more dazed than I feel, and she and Oliver help me to my feet. Oliver holds onto my hand for as long as possible as the paramedic leads me and Bobbie over to an ambulance. As we approach, I see Jiminy sitting on the edge of the open back, a blanket wrapped around his shoulders as a male paramedic notes down his vitals on a chart.

"Haley!" He gets to his feet, ignoring the paramedic trying to urge him to sit back down.

Jiminy staggers over to me and takes my face in his hands, the smell of smoke sticks to us both like a second skin. He's full-on crying now, even worse than my sister.

"You stupid, brave girl. How dare you try to save this old geezer first instead of yourself? I don't know what I would've done if—" a sob catches in his throat and he pulls me to his chest.

Without even thinking for a moment I wrap my arms around him and finally let my own tears fall.

"I couldn't just leave you," I whisper against his chest. "I couldn't leave you there."

He holds me tight, one hand patting my back as the other cradles my head. "I know, my dear. I know." I feel his head shift as Bobbie comes to stand beside me. "Your sister is a very brave witch," he says softly.

I can't see Bobbie's face from where my own is buried in Jiminy's chest, but through the sorella magica I can tell she's shocked that he knows.

It's another several minutes until the paramedic is done taking my vitals and I'm staring at the charred remains of *Jiminy's Oddities* that something Jiminy said to me amidst the blaze flashes bright in my mind.

I always knew it.

He knew all along that I was a witch and he never thought of me any differently.

Scary Ghost Stories & Tales of The Glories Of Christmases Long Long Ago

Oliver gives me a nervous smile as he sits down beside me on the park bench. When he asked to meet, I knew I couldn't risk him coming over or vice versa because then we would just end up in bed and what I have to tell him is too important to brush past and too extreme to talk about in the close confines of the coffee shop or pub.

"Hi, sweetheart."

He wraps an arm around my shoulders and pulls me in close, planting a gentle kiss on top of my head. His pine needle, smoky scent washes over me and my heart hurts at the mere thought of what I'm about to say.

"What's up?" he asks. "You said you wanted to tell me something."

I shift slightly to face him. "Yes but first, isn't there something you want to ask me?"

His brows crinkle a bit, his mouth forms a straight line, it's obvious the curiosity has been nagging at him but he hasn't brought it up yet, probably trying to think of a logical explanation for what happened at Jiminy's the other day.

"It's okay," I urge. "You can ask."

He reaches out and takes one of my hands in his, my palms and wrists are inflamed so the chilly touch of his fingers provides some relief.

"How did you get Jiminy out of the building? He kept saying that you saved him, that you got him out. How is that possible? You were both on the second floor and the doorway was blocked."

"I saved him with magic."

He's quiet for a moment then he laughs nervously. "What do you mean?"

"I mean that I'm about to tell you something ridiculous." I pause for a moment, giving him a chance to stop me, to call me crazy and walk away. But he doesn't. He just waits patiently for me to continue. "I'm a descendant of La Befana, The Good Witch of Christmas. The reason I don't have an Italian or Greenlandic accent is because I was raised at The North Pole."

Oliver laughs nervously. "The North Pole is just ice, isn't it?"

"The one mortals can access, yes. I grew up at The Terrestrial North Pole. The portal is through a cottage on Kaffeklubben, the island off the coast of Greenland I told you about. My mother abandoned me and my sister there when she realized we were witches. The magic skipped her generation and she and my father wanted a normal Christian life. They hated witches so they disowned us as children and left us to be raised by our grandfather, Babbo Natale."

An awful silence hangs over us. I hold my breath, ready for the inevitable pain of him calling me crazy. I've never told anyone I'm a witch, I know better. I've been thinking about what Jiminy said over and over again: *I always knew it.* It's given me a sliver of foolish hope that maybe Oliver will believe me.

"Babbo Natale?" Oliver asks.

I nod. "It's Italian."

"For?"

"Santa Claus."

He laughs again, his eyes darting around my face, clearly waiting for me to laugh too and admit it's all a joke.

"Haley, are you telling me that your grandfather is Santa Claus and you grew up at—what? Santa's Workshop?"

"There's more than just a workshop at The Terrestrial North Pole. There's a whole village."

His laughter turns into a huff of disbelief.

"Haley, listen, I understand the fire was traumatic, and I know what it's like to be trapped in a burning building, you know this, but—"

Before he can finish I reach down and pluck a blade of grass from the ground beneath us. I lay it flat in my palm and focus. The crimson sparks appear around the lines in my palm, dimmer than when I fought the fire, but visible nonetheless. The blade of grass shakes and floats and transforms into a tiny pine tree. I lift my other hand up, hovering it above the top of the tree. More crimson sparks dart out as I move my fingers through perfectly practiced motions and decorations begin to don the tree. Tiny ornaments and garlands, miniature candy canes (even smaller than the ones he delivered), and a sweet-faced small angel sits on the top. I look up from my creation to meet Oliver's eyes. His mouth hangs agape as he stares transfixed at the magic before him.

With a resigned sigh, I snap my fingers and the tree turns to gold and red dust that floats back down to the ground from whence it came. Oliver watches it fall before looking back at me.

"Haley, I don't know—"

"I was having a bad pain flare the other day," I say. "It took all my energy to get Jiminy out. Usually, I would've been able to use my magic to get myself out of the building too but I was just so drained. I just...Jiminy told me to save myself but I couldn't leave him."

Oliver reaches out for one of my hands again, I let him take it, comforted once again by the chill of his skin.

"Your parents they..."

"People hate witches, even if they don't believe we exist."

Oliver's gaze saddens; somehow the pity hurts worse than if he were to just call me crazy.

"My grandfather didn't really pay much attention to us growing up. I used to send my mother Christmas cards, but they always got sent back unopened. I barely even remember my parents, I was so little when they gave us up. La Befana, my great-grandmother, was the only family who seemed to really care about us. Bobbie and I came here to have a nice, normal life together. Bobbie fell in love and got married and then her husband Christopher died in the car crash and *I* was the one who was driving. So you see, I couldn't leave Jiminy behind. I couldn't just save myself."

Oliver squeezes my hand. "What are you trying to say?"

I drop his hand and grab my cane from where I propped it on the other side of the fence.

"I'm saying I'll only complicate your life the way I've complicated everyone else's."

"Haley, wait." Oliver reaches up and grabs my arm as I start to leave. "I don't care that you're a witch. I don't care that you're disabled."

I nod once, biting my lip, fighting back tears in my eyes. "But you will one day. I know it."

He shakes his head fervently.

"I loved someone once," I whisper. "But she cared that I was a witch. I've tried to fall in love since and they all cared that I was disabled. I'm the reason my sister has lost so much. *I'm* the reason I'm disabled. I'm—"

Oliver gets to his feet and takes hold of my shoulders. "You didn't make the car crash."

That's what Bobbie and Ati Nanca always tell me. But it's become impossible to believe. My darkest hours have come to claim me once more and I can't bear risking bringing any more unhappiness upon someone I care about. Better to cut the cord and let Oliver go before he's in too deep.

"I have to go," I say softly. "I'm sorry."

I pull free of his grasp and head home. I was scheduled to work today, but even that's gone now.

———

La Befana is waiting for me when I get home, tea already prepared.

"You really are a foolish woman," she tells me.

I discard my coat, purse, and cane and come over to sit beside her, Charlie Chaplin purring between us.

"Care to elaborate?"

"Your sister tells me you've fallen in love with a nice firefighter."

"I never told her that."

Ati Nanca laughs. "You know you don't have to *tell* Bobbie anything for her to know it."

I sigh as I reach for my tea. It's cooled enough since she made it that I can tolerate a sip. There's not enough sugar, but I swallow the bitter taste anyway.

"Why do you insist on punishing yourself for things that are not your fault?" Ati Nanca asks.

"I don't—"

"It is not your fault that your mother and father were cruel, unloving people. It is not your fault that even fairies and elves judge witches and that my stupid son wasn't a good enough guardian to you. If anything, my darling, that one is *my* fault."

"You couldn't raise us. You're La Befana. You can't stay stationary."

"I *know* that." She looks down her nose at me. "I still could have done more. But you have always done the most to move through this life with a loving heart despite the darkness and cruelty of others that has followed you. That is something admirable. That is something brave."

I drop my gaze to the mug balancing on my lap. "I'm not brave."

She grabs my chin and tilts my head back up, her fierce eyes boring into me. "No one is meaner to you than *you*, Haley. And now you've found yourself someone you want to spend your time with and you're going to deny yourself that happiness? Why? Because you don't want him to know you're a witch?"

"I told him I'm a witch."

Ati Nanca huffs and releases my chin. "Then what's the problem? Why can't you let yourself be happy?"

Tears blur my vision. "Because," I whisper. "I think I hate myself."

"Oh, my dear." She reaches out and places a hand on my shoulder, gently rubbing her thumb back and forth. "You're the only one who does."

"I feel like...I'm not something anyone would want.."

She grips my shoulder. "You listen to me, Haley Rossi. *I* want you. Your sister and niece want you. And it sounds like this firefighter wants you too."

I wipe away some of my tears. "I haven't told you anything about him."

She gives me a wise smile. "I'm The Good Witch of Christmas, dear. When it comes to Christmas magic, nothing gets past me."

"It's not Christmas magic, Ati Nanca."

"My dear, darling girl, love is the greatest magic of all."

And When I'm Feeling Alone You Remind Me Of Home. Oh, Baby Baby, Merry Christmas

It's Christmas Eve Eve. Tomorrow night is family dinner with Bobbie, Noelle, Ati Nanca, and Jiminy. It feels odd to have seen Ati Nanca so much this year prior to the holiday. I called Bobbie after Ati Nanca left last night and asked her again if the witch had visited her at all.

"She only stopped by after the fire to ask about you," Bobbie said. "She's been worried. So have I."

"You don't need to worry about me," I told her.

"We're witches, Haley. A coven. It's what we do."

I laughed, smiling against the phone. "We're hardly a coven, Bobbie."

"Maybe not, but we are family."

Now I'm sitting on my couch staring at the Christmas lights I used magic to string up around my apartment. My body is still recovering from the pain flare and the fire so doing it physically wasn't an option. Besides, it feels good to use my magic so much again.

I bought a nice bottle of red wine and a gingerbread scented candle. I take a deep breath and tell myself this is for the best. I light the candle then take out my new phone, snap a picture, and send it to Oliver.

> There's a fire in my apartment. I need a firefighter.

I sit in anxiety for a few minutes but then the typing dots appear and he responds.

> On my way.

I get up and pace nervously, my knees clicking and burning but I ignore the pain. Charlie Chaplin meows at me in confusion a few times before deciding to ignore my erratic behavior and curling up to go to sleep. Another few minutes of insanity passes and then there's a knock on my door.

Oliver stands on the other side, face flushed from the cold, peacoat only half buttoned.

"Hi," I say softly.

"Hey."

I move to the side so he can come in. I close the door as he walks over to the coffee table in front of the couch and picks up the candle. He turns back to face me and holds my gaze as he blows out the flame. I offer a small smile in return.

"My hero."

He laughs softly, his mouth curving up into that beautiful smile of his, his eyes shining like stars.

I take a step closer to him. "I'm sorry for pushing you away. I think I'm so afraid of someone not wanting me or someone leaving me that I end up leaving them before I have a chance to get hurt. It's stupid, I know."

Oliver shakes his head, walking back over to me, closing out the space between us and taking my hands in his own. It hasn't been that long since we held hands on the bench and yet I missed feeling his touch so ardently.

"It's not stupid," he says. He looks me in the eye and raises one hand up to cup my cheek, his fingers stroking along my jaw. He takes a slow, deep breath before he speaks again. "You know how I told you I was in a fire as a kid."

I nod. "Your apartment."

"Right. Well, the fire was my fault. I set it. Not on purpose, but still."

"What happened?"

"I was a little kid, my dad liked to get drunk and pass out on the sofa or just stay out late with different friends and girl-friends, leaving me at home to fend for myself. Sometimes I think he got so fucked up he forgot he even had a kid. Not one he wanted anyway. So, one night he came home late, wasted, and passed out on the couch. There weren't any snacks or even anything I could easily get. So I decided to try and make some food myself. I don't even remember what I was trying to make, just that I set a fire with the stove. I didn't get any fire safety from my dad so I had no idea what to do. I tried to wake him but he was out cold. Even the smell of his home burning didn't rouse him, he was so fucked up."

"So what did you do?" I whisper.

He slides his hand back to tangle his fingers in my hair, holding my head steady, keeping my gaze locked on his.

"I remembered a teacher at school mentioning 911, to call it if we needed help. I found my dad's cell phone and did that. They were able to save us, but CPS got involved and deemed my dad unfit to raise me. They took me away and put me in foster care. I tried to reach out to him over the years, just like you did with your mom. But I never heard back. So, you see, I know what it feels like to be abandoned; to feel unwanted. I understand that part of you, Haley. And while I may not understand what it's like to live with chronic pain or um... *magic.*"

He laughs a little on the word and the sound brings a smile to my face. His fingers stroke through my hair, tenderly massaging the base of my scalp, soothing some of my pain. I move closer to him and rest my hands on his chest, letting him be my anchor amidst this tempestuous sea.

"But I *want* to be here and listen and learn." He ducks his head down a bit so we're at eye level and moves his hands to hold my face in his palms. I curl my fingers into the fabric of his shirt, letting him steady me, letting him hold me. "I want to be with you, Haley. I want to—" he takes a nervous breath and laughs through the exhale. "I want to fall in love with you."

I shift forward onto my toes, my nose grazing against his, my breath warm against his lips.

"I want that too," I breathe.

Oliver's smile brightens and then his mouth is on mine. He tightens his grip on my face and I move my hands to hold onto his forearms, pulling him down closer to me. We simultaneously make the decision to start tearing away at each other's clothes as we stumble over to my bed. Once we're both clad in only our undergarments Oliver takes a step back and just stares at me. I'm wearing a lace set of a red bra and panties, both of which leave *very* little up to the imagination.

"I just thought..." I flush all over under his gaze. "Well... you know. Merry Christmas."

Oliver grins and practically pounces on me, shoving me back onto the bed so hard I squeak in surprise. He grinds against me, the pressure of his erection creating friction against my core even through the fabric of our underwear. He drops his mouth down to kiss and bite my neck, swiping his tongue and teeth over every possible sensitive area he can find. I dig my fingers into his back and drag my nails down, eliciting a groan from deep in his throat.

"God, Haley, the things I want to do to you. If you'd let me."

I move my hands to his hair and push it back so I can see his starry eyes perfectly.

"I'd let you."

He chuckles. "You might not want to be so quick to answer, sweetheart."

I lift myself up a bit and press my lips to his ear. I lightly blow air directly into his ear, causing him to shudder. I smile against the shell of his ear before taking his earlobe in my mouth and biting down. He groans and thrusts his hips against mine.

"Tell me," I whisper.

He pushes himself up onto his forearms to look down at me, his bright eyes shining under the colorful glow of the Christmas lights strung up above us.

"If I'm being honest, sweetheart, I'd like to tie you up, bend you over this bed, spank your ass until it's as red as these panties—" he reaches down to cup my cunt in the palm of his hand as he says this, causing me to gasp loudly and his grin to broaden. "—and then fuck your from behind. *But* I don't have any rope with me and I doubt you do either. Plus, I don't want to make your rheumatoid arthritis flare up."

My pulse is racing just from his words. It feels like it's been ages since I've engaged in the kind of volatile, intense sex he's describing. Most people I've hooked up with over the years have always been rather put off by my propositions of wanting to be dominated, and once my chronic pain worsened the reality of most men's lazy attitude toward aftercare became far too evident and detrimental to my health.

But somehow I know Oliver is different from all the rest.

"If you're willing to massage me after, then I won't flare up tomorrow." *At least not so badly that it wouldn't be worth it.*

I run my fingers through his hair again, loving the way his eyes flutter closed and his jaw goes slack when I do. "Plus, I thought I made it clear when we had sex the first time, I like a little pain."

Oliver kisses me as he shoves one hand under the cup of my bra and roughly pinches my nipple until I whimper against his mouth, but I don't ask him to stop.

"But, sweetheart, this would be more than just a little pain."

"I want it," I rasp against his mouth. "I want everything you want to give me."

"We still don't have rope."

Without giving myself a moment to second guess it, I wave my hand in the air, fingers swiping back and forth to loosen and lower one of the strands of Christmas lights. Oliver looks up and watches in awe as I use my magic to guide the decor down to the bed, the warm, colorful bulbs settling around us.

"Christ," Oliver says under his breath.

"Another witch."

He laughs. "Really?"

"Come on, walks on water, water into wine? Be serious."

He laughs again as he kisses me and I swallow the sound. I want to consume every part of him I can. Now that I know what it's like to have him here in my life I want to keep uncovering new parts of him until I've memorized him like all the spells I know by heart.

"Alright, my little heretic." Oliver reaches around me and grabs the strand of lights. He crawls off me and holds a hand out. "Come here."

I take his hand and let him pull me up to stand. He takes my hand and sets the strand of lights in it, the warmth of the bulbs spreading across my palm. Oliver trails his fingers up my arm to come rest along my bra strap. He starts to slide it down my shoulder, eyes never leaving mine.

"You should let me take this off," he whispers.

I nod and turn around slowly. He trails those same tantalizing fingers across my back until he reaches the clasp. He undoes it and takes the strand of lights back so I can let my bra fall to the floor.

"Put your arms behind your back, sweetheart."

I do as he says without question, easily losing myself in the feeling of giving myself over to him. I know I'm safe with him. I know he will take care of me through all the pain and pleasure.

Oliver begins to bind my arms behind my back with the strand of lights, the bulbs warming my skin, the cord lightly digging into my skin. He ties them tight enough that I'm not completely uncomfortable but it won't be easy for me to get free on my own. He presses a hand between my shoulder blades and pushes me down onto the bed. I shiver in anticipation as he drags his fingers down my spine until he reaches the waistband of my panties. The idea of getting to be fucked from behind again without having to worry about killing my knees on the bed is exciting to me but the fact that we're delving deeper into the depravity of taboo pleasures sends the butterflies inside me into heat, their papery wings bursting into blooming flames that lick across my ribcage and travel lower and *lower*.

"Spread your legs for me, sweetheart."

I shift as much as I can in my bound position to accommodate his command. Once my stance is wide enough Oliver presses his hand to my sex, feeling the wetness seeping through the thin fabric of my lace underwear.

"God, you're so fucking sexy, Haley."

He begins to work his fingers back and forth, driving me mad with the slightest touch. I suddenly feel the pressure of his body on top of mine. He pushes my hair to one side and whispers in my ear: "I'm going to spank you now. Tell me to stop if it's too much."

He stands back up, leaving me breathless and before I fully have time to process what's about to happen he brings his hand down hard across my ass. I gasp loudly and buck against the mattress, the sting of his palm spreading across my skin.

"Should I keep going?"

I nod against the mattress, still trying to get my bearings in the wake of the sweet pain.

Oliver spanks me again and this time I cry out.

"Use your words, Haley."

I can hear the smirk in his words.

"Yes, Oliver," I breathe. "Keep going."

"Okay, sweetheart."

He knots one hand in my hair and uses the other to spank me over and over again as my body convulses and my arms strain against my yuletide-themed bondage. He keeps spanking me, alternating between one ass cheek and the other, letting the smarting pain spread and sink in deep. After I think I can't take anymore and my core feels soaked he yanks the fabric up, roughly dragging it against me, pulling the material taut against my slit and dragging another gasp from my mouth. With my bare skin now exposed he resumes his spanking anew, making sure to distribute his blows thoroughly.

"Had enough yet, little heretic?"

"I don't know, firefighter," I pant. "Do you have more to give?"

He chuckles and yanks my panties all the way down to my knees.

"Tis the season of giving, Haley." He tugs on the elastic band. "Step out of these."

I do as he says until I'm completely bare before him. He digs his nails into my ass, kneading roughly, massaging my reddened flesh. I moan and bury my face into the mattress. He starts to spank me again, this time making sure to spank every inch of my ass, the sides, the swell where my cheeks meet my thighs, and just when I'm about to cry out that I can't take anymore he switches to spanking my thighs and then my cunt. The heat from his hand blends with the heat of the lights and I scream, writhing and wet.

"Oliver, please!"

"Please what, sweetheart?" He doesn't relent in his spanking, his palm making contact over and over again with my cunt.

"Please fuck me."

"Gladly."

The sound of his palm hitting my skin stops and is replaced by the sound of a condom wrapper tearing open. He lines his length up with my entrance, his body brushing up against mine. His strong hands take hold of my hips and then he slams me back onto his cock so hard I see stars almost as bright as the ones in his eyes. I moan louder and louder with every rutting thrust he gives me. My arms struggle against their binds, my core thrums, my face flushes, my heart soars.

"You're so perfect, Haley."

He slows his thrust and dips down to kiss me between my shoulders. He trails more kisses across my back, down along my spine and back up again. When he reaches my neck he starts to use his tongue, moving the muscle in time with his thrusts.

"Oliver," I whimper. "I'm so close."

He picks up the pace again, pistoning his hips against mine, his cock burrowing deep inside me, the pace punishing, the sensation insanity inducing.

"Come for me, little heretic."

He lands a few more spanks to my ass in time with his hips, body slapping against mine, and an orgasm like a tornado whirls through my body, stealing a cry so loud from my throat that Oliver has to cover my mouth with his hand so the neighbors don't suspect I'm being murdered in here.

I moan against his palm as he keeps fucking me, chasing that euphoria I'm eager to give him. I move my hips as much as I can from my compromised position, but much like last time all I can do is give myself over to the power and the pleasure of his body.

It feels so good to let someone have control, to not have to be constantly taking stock of my body—my pain. It feels so freeing to give the reins over to someone else and let them guide me through every sensation.

With a final thrust and a deep groan Oliver finishes, his body slumping over mine.

After a few heavy shared breaths I wiggle a bit beneath him.

"Oliver, take these off."

"Right, right, of course."

He pulls out of me slowly and gets to work undoing my holiday binds. He helps me turn around and lay back on the bed, my entire body flushed and thoroughly spent.

"Wait right here." He kisses my forehead and walks to the bathroom.

I watch him disappear behind the door and then reemerge, having disposed of the condom and carrying a bottle of ibuprofen in one hand. He goes into the kitchenette and fills a glass with water then returns to me.

"Will these help?"

I smile and nod. "A little, yeah. Help me sit up?"

Oliver does as I ask and opens the bottle for me. He shakes out two pills into my hand and I smirk.

"More?" He raises a brow in disbelief.

"This isn't amateur hour, darling."

"Mmm, darling." He kisses me quickly before shaking out two more pills. "I like how that sounds, sweetheart."

I take the pills and the glass of water. "What? No more 'little heretic'?"

I take a gulp of water and swallow the pills easily in one go from years of painful practice.

Oliver takes the glass and sets it aside on the nightstand. "I think I'll reserve that one for special occasions." He kisses me again. "Now, tell me how I can help. I don't want you to be in pain tomorrow. The bad kind of pain, that is."

I laugh softly. I can't seem to stop smiling.

"Are you any good at giving massages?" I ask.

"I think I can hold my own."

"Well then." I lay back and roll over onto my stomach. "Be my guest, *darling*."

Oliver wastes no time in moving his hands to my body. For the next half hour he thoroughly massages every inch of me until I'm a pool of relaxation.

"Let's get some sleep," I murmur against my pillow.

"Good idea."

Oliver curls up beside me under the covers and holds me tight as the winter winds blow outside my window. I snap my fingers and the Christmas lights go out, Oliver laughs against my neck.

"I don't know if I'll ever get used to this whole magic thing," he says.

I lace my fingers with his. "You've got time."

He kisses my neck, I can feel the smile on his lips as he does. I reach up and touch the pendant still hanging around my neck. I let the calming magic radiate off it until I drift off to sleep in the arms of the man I plan to fall in love with.

I'll Be Home For Christmas

The doorbell rings as Bobbie is pulling the pies out of the oven.

"I'll get it!" I call out.

I open the door, expecting to see Ati Nanca, but instead Oliver is standing there, beaming, holding a small, wrapped box.

"Oliver, what are you—"

"I invited him." I turn around to see my sister smiling at me, wiping her hands on a dish towel. "Come in, Oliver, please. Dinner's almost ready. We're just waiting on our Ati Nanca."

Oliver steps inside and closes the door behind him. "Ati Nanca?"

"Etruscan for grandmother."

"Um, Etruscan?"

"Right." I shake my head and lead him toward the dining room. "It's what people spoke in Italy before it was Italy. My great-grandmother, La Befana, is from Italy. That is all true, my Italian heritage. So we call her Ati Nanca."

"Can you speak Etruscan?"

I laugh. "Please, I can barely speak Italian. What's in the box?"

We come to the dining room door. I can hear Noelle inside setting down plates while explaining to Jiminy the kind of pies she helped Bobbie bake, and I can feel the change in the air that means Ati Nanca is close. In a few hours, the sound of sleigh bells will ring out from the roof as my grandfather comes to deliver gifts to Noelle. Christmas draws near and for the first time in a long time I'm not miserable about the idea.

"Oh." Oliver looks down at the box. "It's for you."

I smile and take the box from him, gently pulling back the wrapping. I open it up to find a taxidermy dove inside. I gasp at the beautiful piece of art and gently take it out and hold the creature in my hand, forever preserved in a moment of beauty.

"Thank you," I breathe, looking up at Oliver.

Oliver leans down and kisses my forehead, letting his hand rest gently against the back of my head. I close my eyes and lean into his sweet touch.

"Merry Christmas, Haley."

The air whirls and shifts as Ati Nanca appears before us. Oliver gasps, startled. La Befana just smiles at him with that mischievous look in her eye.

"Well, don't just stand there gawking," she tells him. "We're going to be late for dinner."

She marches past us into the dining room, the heady scent of cinnamon and cloves following in her wake. Oliver turns to follow but I reach out and grab his sleeve.

"Before I forget." I reach into my pocket and take out a candy cane. "Special delivery."

THE END

Acknowledgments

THANK YOU TO...

Marcia Leticia Ruiz-Olguín and Jay Gaunt for helping this story take flight and for hilarious comments on Google docs.

Katy Doyle for reining in my sometimes nonsensical use of semicolons.

Mika, Amanda Nikole, Fern, and Ali for singing the praises of this story in all its absurdity.

Lindsey for being a digital cheerleader without my ever needing to ask, bringing joy to my phone screen on a regular basis.

My mother for helping keep me afloat.

My ADHD for never allowing me to write a chill Christmas romance but rather always insisting I do extensive research on ancient folklore to weave throughout the narrative. You're the one disability of mine that I wouldn't wish away.

YOU, dear reader, for journeying to the fictional world of Huey Maryland and indulging this 911 and witchcraft obsessed Christmas lover to tell this silly tale.

ABOUT THE AUTHOR

Molly Likovich is the Bestselling Author of *Riding The Headless Horseman (Sexy Sleepy Hollow #1),* as well as titles such as *Send in The Clowns* and *There's Something in The Woods.* Her short stories and poetry have appeared in *Love Letters To Poe Vol. 3, The New Mexico Review,* and *Rust + Moth* among many others. She has a Bachelor's in Creative Writing from Salisbury University and currently lives in her Maryland hometown with her chaotic dogs. Learn more about her at mollylikovich.com

ALSO BY MOLLY LIKOVICH

Riding The Headless Horseman (Sexy Sleepy Hollow #1)

Getting With The Ghoul (Sexy Sleepy Hollow #2)

There's Something in The Woods

Send in The Clowns

Loved Alone

Falling for Jack Frost

Be Terrible

Lumos & Lattes

By Molly Likovich & Marcia Ruiz-Olguín

Not a Myth (Faoinsguel Woods #1)

The Willow's Silence (Faoinsgeul Woods #2)

The Fable of Wonderland